Two
Little Naughty Beavers

By
Ariadne Winquist

Illustrated by Renae Wallace

Illustrations by Renae Wallace

This Book Belongs to

Beavers play and work together

Once upon a time there was a happy family of beavers. There was a mother and father beaver and two little kits named Alissandra and Aubrie (a kit is the name of a young beaver).

The beaver family worked very hard every day chewing down trees to build their dams. They would build dams by chewing with their great big sharp front teeth, and then pile the trees together to block the water and make the dam. The kits were taught that if they did not chew the trees regularly their teeth would grow way down over their chins so far in fact, that they would not be able to even open their mouth's.

Beavers always face many dangers. The biggest and scariest danger of all is

MAN.

Men, called trappers, make their living by trapping beavers in cages. They use the beaver fur to make tall hats for men and beautiful coats for the ladies. They are able to trick the beavers into going into their traps by tempting them with delicious beaver candy that they place right in the center of the cages.

One day, Alissandra and Aubrie decided to pretend that they were sick so that they would not have to go to work! Alissandra said to Aubrie, "let's stay home and just play all day in the water.   I think we can fool mother."   And they did.

Alissandra and Aubrie had sooooo much fun that they decided to play sick again the next day and even the third day, too. The parents agreed to let them stay home because they really did seem sick but they must promise to never go into the woods by their lodge. They explained that beaver hunters might be out there trapping and they wanted their kits to be safe. The girls promised to not go into the woods by slapping their big fat tails

After a couple of days of splashing around in the water, Alissandra and Aubrie got bored and thought it might be more fun and exciting to explore the forbidden woods.

They agreed to keep it a secret from their mom and dad. They figured it would be OK if they were very, very careful.

Oh my goodness what fun they had in the woods. This was much better than chewing down trees. The kits were gone so long that they even had to go potty so they just went right there in the woods. They made funny giggling sounds as they left traces of poo all through the woods.

All of a sudden, they realized that they were lost! They were so lost that they couldn't even find their way back to their lodge. The two kits were getting

tired, hungry and very frightened as they frantically began looking for something familiar. It was then that they saw a most interesting object with something inside that was very pretty and smelled really good. What they didn't realize was that they were looking at the MAN TRAP!

Their eyes just sparkled when they spotted beaver candy right in the middle of that thing. They got so excited that they ran right into it and started trying to eat the delicious sugar treats when suddenly the cage door slammed shut and They were trapped inside.

What was even worse, they couldn't even eat the candy because their teeth had grown long. They had grown so gradually that they didn't realize that they couldn't open their mouths. As they sat there looking at each other they noticed it was getting dark and they started to cry. Alissandra and Aubrie wanted their mommy and daddy.

They wished that they had listened to the rules about straying far from home. All at once Aubrie got an idea and explained her plan to Alissandra via sign language. She remembered when they slapped their tails real hard that the slapping sound could be heard from very far away. In fact, this is how they talk to each other. So, they decided to slap their tails hard against the metal floor of the cage three times in a row. They hoped that maybe their parents might hear them. Aubrie motioned 123, SLAP, SLAP, SLAP again, SLAP SLAP SLAP. They did this over and over until they felt their tails would break right off.

While the kits were making as much noise as they could, their mom and dad were back home searching for them. They were scared and just knew that the hunters would capture their girls and they would never see them again. The kits were way too far away for mom and dad to hear their frantic slaps calling for help.

It was getting darker and darker and their mom and dad had been swimming and searching the ponds all around their lodge but could not find a trail. Then they decided to search the forbidden woods just in case the kits thought it would be safe. Immediately they smelled the scent of their little beaver poos.

It wasn't long before they were greeted with the sound of tails slapping, SLAP, SLAP, SLAP. They followed the sounds and smells as quickly as they could and behold they found their kits. However, their joy faded when they saw that their precious kits were trapped inside the MAN CAGE!

OH MY GOSH! Mom and dad knew they had to hurry so they went right to work and broke into the man cage. After freeing Alissandra and Aubrie, the family quickly jumped into the nearby pond and swam home. They did not even stop to hug each other because they knew that every minute counted if they wanted to get home safely.

At that very moment the beaver man trappers were quietly approaching their trap. Too bad they arrived so late. The trappers missed them by just a few minutes. They never even saw their flat tails disappear beneath the surface of the water. The beavers made their escape home just in the nick of time

The beavers were so happy to be safe and all together in their cozy lodge that They hugged and kissed and hugged and kissed (beaver hugs and kisses of Course). Naturally, the kits promised to never disobey their parents again.

However, the next morning mom and dad noticed that the girls could not even open their mouth a tiny little bit. The fact that they had not gone to work and chewed down trees made their teeth grow way down past their chins.

Oh my, oh my, what on earth can they do?

Of course, mom and dad beaver had a great plan as all parents do. They took the girls downstream to their favorite dentist, Dr. Chops.

Dr. chops filed their teeth down with the file that was made just for beaver teeth. When he was done he asked the kits to promise that they would obey their parents in the future. And they did. Well, most of the time.

And of course, they all lived happily ever after

The End

Beavers play and work together

Ten Beaver Facts

Beavers have clear eyelids so the can see underwater.

Beaver teeth never stop growing so they MUST gnaw on wood to keep them short.

Beavers are one of the largest rodents on earth.

The lips of a beaver are behind its teeth which help it carry around branches and not drown.

Beavers live in lodges around rivers and lakes.

Beavers are nocturnal.

Beavers have strong jaws and teeth.

Beavers have thick fur and webbed feet.

Beavers have flat tails covered with scales.

Beavers Teeth are coated with iron so they look orange.

About The Author

Ariadne is 85 and a resident of Cedar Springs Michigan. She earned her BA degree from Aquinas college and is a mother of four, grandmother of nine and a great grandmother of 12. The inspiration for the beaver story was created when she was asked to make up stories at bedtime for her youngest grandchildren, Alissandra and Aubrie.

After a few years of telling the beaver story, her daughter Bonita encouraged her to write it down for publication. "I wouldn't have done it without her encouragement"

Drawing  Page

Drawing

Page

Drawing  Page

Made in the USA
Monee, IL
07 May 2020